Go Home, Little One!

For the other Hedgehog, and my Mouse.
With lots of love.
CJ

Quarto is the authority on a wide range of topics.
Quarto educates, entertains and enriches the lives of
our readers—enthusiasts and lovers of hands-on living.
www.quartoknows.com

Paperback edition first published in 2017
First published in hardback in the UK in 2015 by
words & pictures, an imprint of Quarto Publishing Plc,
The Old Brewery, 6 Blundell Street, London N7 9BH

British Library Cataloguing in Publication Data available on request

ISBN 978-1-91027-721-8

1 3 5 7 9 8 6 4 2

Printed in China

Go Home, Little One!

Cate James

words & pictures

Florence and Mrs Hedgehog lived in the
bottom of a tall tree, deep in the forest.
   The squirrel twins, Harry and Barry, lived
upstairs.
   It was almost winter, and some animals
were getting ready for their long winter sleep.

Florence loved spring . . .

. . . Florence loved summer . . .

. . . and Florence loved autumn.

But she didn't know if she loved winter, because Florence always slept right through it.

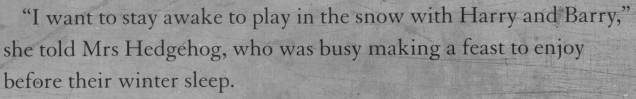

"I want to stay awake to play in the snow with Harry and Barry," she told Mrs Hedgehog, who was busy making a feast to enjoy before their winter sleep.

"You can play with Harry and Barry for a little while," said Mrs Hedgehog, "but don't go too far. We have to get ready to hibernate."

So Florence ran outside to play
hide-and-seek with the squirrel twins.

The three friends
scampered deep
into the forest.
"What are you doing out here?"
Mrs Rabbit asked the three friends.
"It's going to snow soon. You should go home."

But Florence and the twins were having
way too much fun to go home.
They skipped even deeper into the forest.
Sure enough, it began to snow.
Florence loved the soft, white snow, even though
it was cold enough to make her toes tingle.

The three friends built
a huge snow-squirrel.
"It's getting dark," snuffled
Mr Badger. "You should go home."

But Florence and the twins were still having way too much fun to go home.

All of a sudden, it was dark. Even the squirrel twins had never been this far away from home before. The sky was full of snow, and Florence couldn't feel her toes at all!

"Go home!" hooted Mr Owl. "There's danger in these trees. Be careful!"

"N-Not yet!" said Florence, not quite as loudly as before. She wasn't having so much fun anymore.

"Hello, there!" said Mr Fox, showing his pointy teeth. "It's time to eat!"

"I WANT TO GO HOME!" cried Florence.

"So do we!" squeaked Harry and Barry.

Florence and Harry and Barry
ran and ran and ran.

They ran past Mr Owl.
"I'll tell Mr Fox you went a
different way!" he hooted.

They ran past Mr Badger.
"Head towards Mrs Rabbit's home,
over there!" he snuffled.

They ran past Mrs Rabbit.
"You're almost home!" she told
the friends.

Florence thought she knew where they were,
but everything looked the same in the snow.
"What if we can't find home?" she asked
Harry and Barry.

But at last, Harry and Barry shouted,
"Look, Florence! It's our tree!"

Mrs Hedgehog scooped up Florence in a big hug.
"I missed home," Florence said, "and I'm hungry!"

Harry and Barry stayed for the feast, and then it
was time for Florence's winter sleep.

And Florence and Mrs. Hedgehog
slept soundly in their warm tree until spring.

Cate James

Cate studied at the Edinburgh College
of Art. She visits schools, libraries and
galleries to talk about the many books
she has worked on, and to create
drawings with children.

She also works as a mentor for young
illustrators and regularly exhibits
her work at galleries including
the Scottish National Gallery. She
currently lives in Sydney, Australia.